For Francesca, who sees the world
shine through stones. And for the tiny
and the big Mimosa.

Thank you to Tiberio, who inspired
this book, and to Veronica, Manu,
Pata, John B., Béatrice, Sandro,
and Claudia.

On a Magical Do-Nothing Day

Copyright © 2016 by Beatrice Alemagna

Translation by Jill Davis

Library of Congress Control Number: 2016950338

ISBN 978-0-06-265760-2

The artist used gouache, oil, collage, and wax pencils to create the illustrations for this book.

Typography by Amy Ryan

17 18 19 20 21 SCP 10 9 8 7 6 5 4 3 2 1

❖

Originally published in France in 2016 by Albin Michel

First US edition, 2017

BEATRICE ALEMAGNA

ON A MAGICAL
DO-NOTHING DAY

HARPER

An Imprint of HarperCollins Publishers

Here we were again. Me and Mom in the same cabin. The same forest. The same rain. Dad back in the city.

Mom sat at her desk,
quietly writing, while
I destroyed Martians.
Actually, I was just pressing the
same button over and over.

I wished Dad were here.

"What about a break from your game?" Mom growled.
"Is this going to be another day of doing nothing?"

She was right. There was nothing I wanted to do.
Except destroy Martians.

She took the game out of
my hands and hid it, as usual.

I found it, as usual,
and went outside . . .

. . . where it felt like everything in our garden
was hiding from the rain.

I held my game tightly. Maybe it would
protect me from this boring, wet place.

I walked down the hill.

At the bottom of our path, I saw some flat
rocks in the pond.

The rocks were round—like the heads of
the Martians. I wanted to jump on them and
crush them.

Oh no! What did I do? My game fell in the
pond! This COULD NOT be happening to me!

I stuck my hand into the water to grab it. It
was so icy-cold, I screamed.

Without my game, I had nothing to do.

The rain felt like rocks were hitting me.

I was a small tree trapped outside in a hurricane.

Just then, there were four lights, and four huge snails appeared.

"Is there anything to do around here?" I asked them.

"Yes, indeed," they told me.

I reached out and touched their antennae—as soft as Jell-O.
It made me smile.

So I followed them down a path and found dozens of mushrooms. The air was so damp. I knew the smell from when I was small—my grandparents' basement. My cave of treasures.

I felt a sense that there was something special close by. That I was surrounded.

I bent down and dug my fingers into the mud, where a thousand seeds and pellets, kernels, grains, roots, and berries touched my fingers and hands. An underground world full of treasures that I could feel!

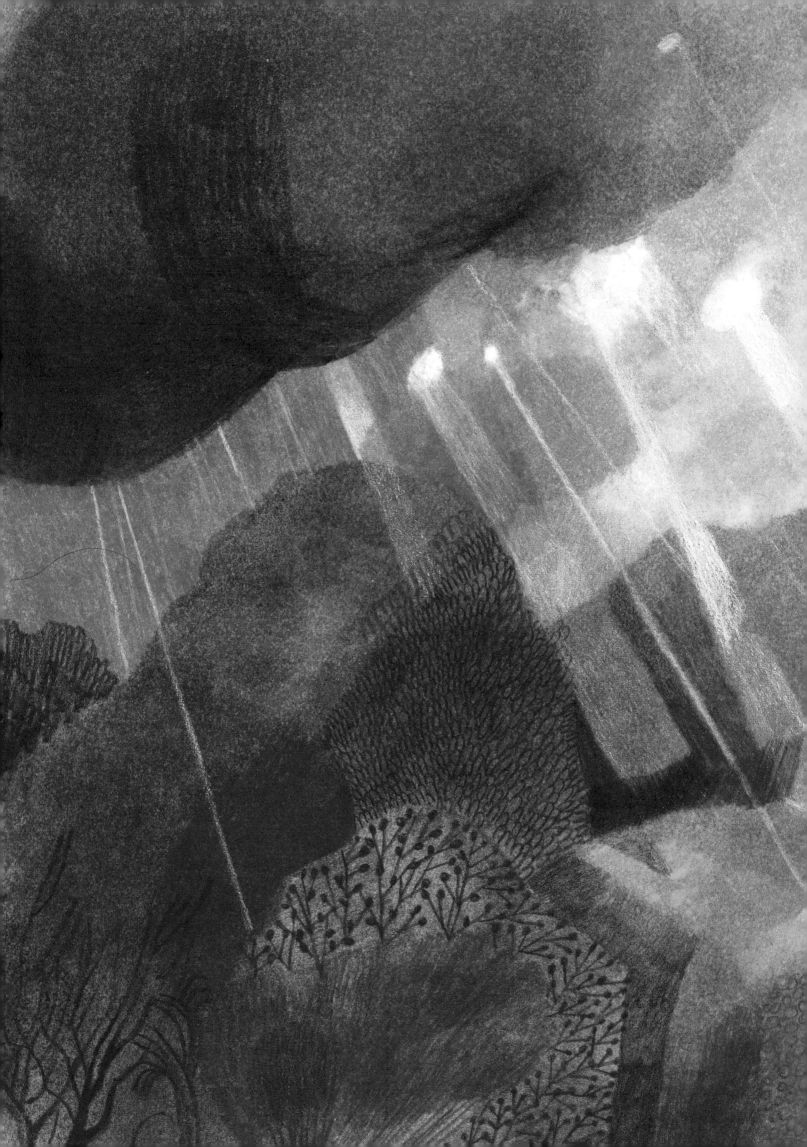

I looked up at the sky. Sunbeams fell down
through a giant strainer and blinded me.

I thought I heard the beat of drums from far away,
but that sound was my heart!

I felt filled up with energy and began running fast.

So fast, I fell down the hill.

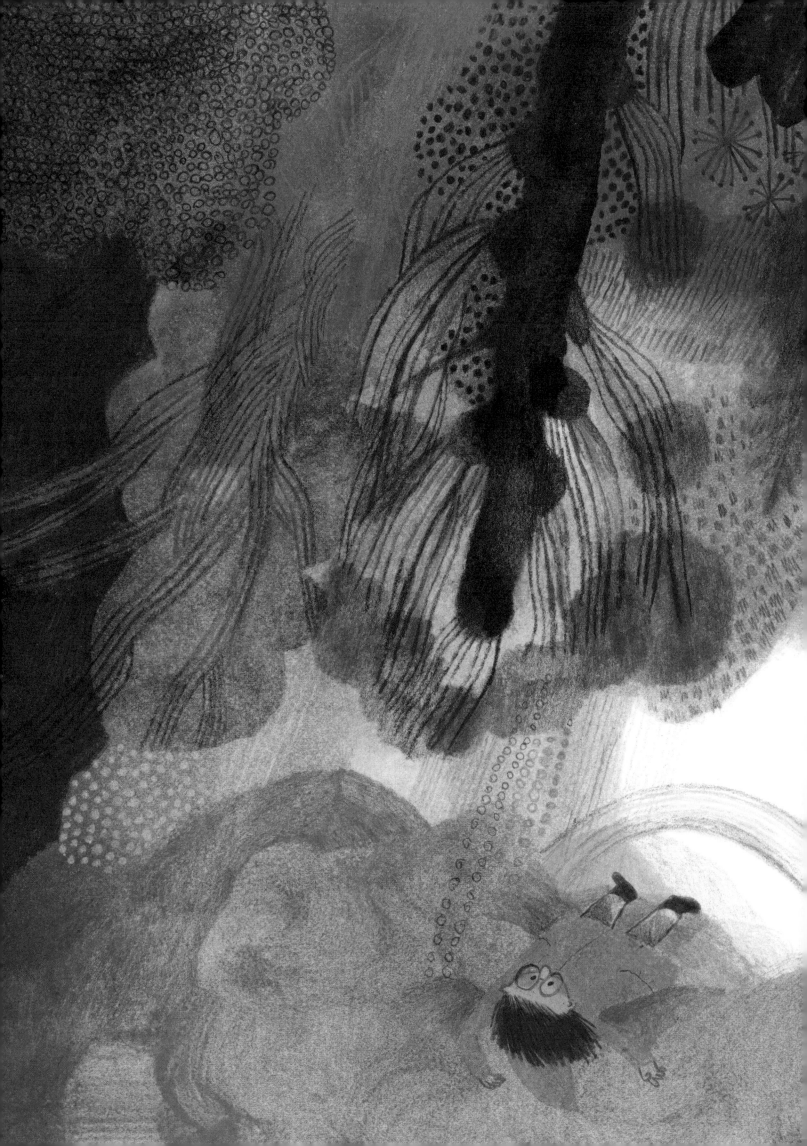

And there at the bottom, everything was turned upside down. The whole world seemed brand-new, as if it had been created right in front of me.

I climbed a tree and looked out
as far as my eyes could see.

I breathed in air until my lungs
were bursting.

I drank the raindrops like an
animal would.

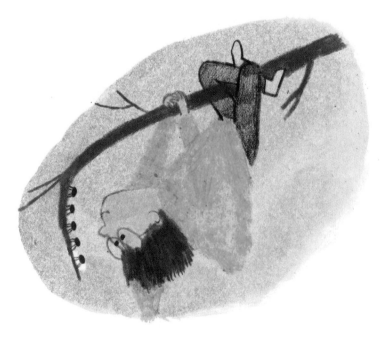

I noticed bugs I'd never seen before.

I talked to a bird.

I made my biggest splash,

then I collected smooth stones as clear as glass
and watched the world shining through them.

Why hadn't I done these things
before today?

Soaked to my bones, I ran inside the house, took off my coat, and looked in the mirror.

Ohhh! I thought I saw my dad smiling at me.

My mother was there, still writing, but now she looked different—like one of the creatures outside.

"Oh! You're soaked. I'll dry you."

She took a towel and brought me to
the kitchen.

I felt like giving her a big hug. I wanted to tell her what I
had seen, felt, and tasted outside in the world.

But I didn't. We just sat in the kitchen, looked at each other, and breathed in the delicious smell of our hot chocolate.

That's it. That's all we did.

On this magical do-nothing day.